SkippyjonJones
IN THE
DOGHOUSE

JUDY SCHACHNER

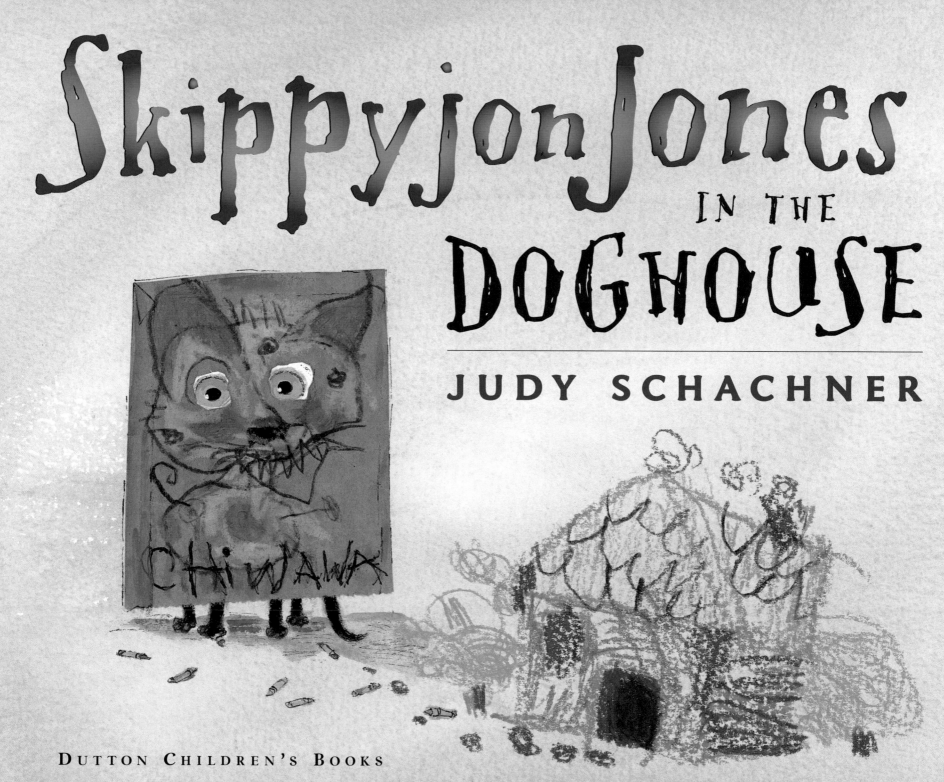

CHIWAWA

DUTTON CHILDREN'S BOOKS

• NEW YORK •

For mis amigos *at the Vanguard School*
and for my brother Kevin—who, at the very
heart of it, is Skippyjon Jones

Con mucho cariño,
    J.B.S.

Library of Congress Cataloging-in-Publication Data
Schachner, Judith Byron.
Skippyjon Jones in the doghouse / by Judith Byron Schachner.—1st ed.
p.   cm.
Summary: Skippyjon Jones is a Siamese cat who wants to be a Chihuahua dog.
ISBN 0-525-47297-5
[1. Siamese cat—Fiction. 2. Cats—Fiction. 3. Chihuahua (Dog breed)—Fiction.
4. Dogs—Fiction.] I. Title.
PZ7.S3286Sk 2005   [E]—dc22   2004017443

Published in the United States by Dutton Children's Books,
a division of Penguin Young Readers Group
345 Hudson Street, New York, New York 10014
www.penguin.com/youngreaders

Designed by Heather Wood

Manufactured in China   •   First Edition
10 9 8 7 6 5 4 3 2 1

The illustrations for this book were created in acrylics
and pen and ink on Aquarelle Arches watercolor paper.

Between the hours of 1 P.M. and 3 P.M., Skippyjon Jones
created his finest piece of artwork ever.

It went up and down and
all around the newly painted
hall. And this rubbed his
mama's fur the wrong way.

"Drop that crayon right now, Mr. Doodlepaws,"
commanded Mama Junebug Jones.
"You're not the boss of me," said Skippyjon Jones.
"In your dreams, Mr. Beans," said Mama.

"I cannot believe that in two quiet hours you covered the walls with those cockeyed Chihuahuas," she scolded. "You are not a Chihuahua. You are a naughty Siamese cat. And you need a time-out to think about that."

The kitty boy did not budge.

But Junebug could be very *purr*-suasive.

"If you think

more like a **cat**,"

she said, "Mama will catch you

a **mouse** big and fat.

I'll dip it in butter

and roll it in

cheese. . . .

All you must do is think

Siamese!"

"And stay out of your closet or
you'll really be in the doghouse,"
she added, putting him into his room.

In fact, Skippyjon Jones was thinking
before Mama Junebug Jones even left.

He was thinking of bouncing. "Doghouse," repeated Skippyjon Jones, beginning to bounce.

First he **bounced** high,

then he **bounced**

low,

pointing his rear to the chair down below.

"Everyone knows
From my big ears to my toes,
I'm not a Siamese cat.
I'm **Skippyjonjones**,
A Chihuahua to my bones.
And that's what I think about that."

But he missed the chair and went careening
into a pile of stuffed animals.

"HOLY Jalapeño!" exclaimed Skippyjon Jones, pulling a bird from his ear.
"The leetle bird says there is a Bobble-ito in the doghouse."

Quicker than you can say *Skippyjonjones Skippyjonjones Skippyjonjones*, the kitty boy climbed into his mask and cape. Then, using his very best Spanish accent, he began to sing.

"Oh, my name is Skippito Friskito.   (clap-clap)

And I heard from a leetle birdito   (clap-clap)

That the doggies have fled

From the gobbling head

Who goes by the name Bobble-ito!"

(clap-clap)

Down the hall, Mama and the girls squeezed together on the couch for a little TV.

"Can Skippyjon watch *Quiz Kitties* with us?" asked Jilly Boo.

"Not right now, pigeon puff," answered Mama. "Skipper-doodle still has some serious Siamese thinking to do."

But Skippyjon Jones
was not thinking Siamese.
He was thinking Chihuahua.

Quiet as a cotton ball, Skippito rolled into his closet. He blew past a boulder, chugged up a hill, and arrived alongside a shack perched two bones shy of the end of the world.

"Where the heckito am I?" wondered Skippito aloud. The place bloomed with sniffing noses.

"Who wants to know?" growled a voice from inside.

"It ees I, El Skippito Friskito, the great sword fighter, the Great Bumblebeeto eater, the great fly defeater, the great spider biter, the greatest *poco perrito* of all," said Skippito.

NO VACANCY

DIG INN

Suddenly a rope cut the air with a
SNAP-ito!
and wrapped around his paw.
"Whoa!" said Skippito as he flew
under the curtain and into the shack.

The house was chock-full of Chihuahuas.

They were cavorting in the
cupboards and splashing
in the sink.

They were chilling in the ice-cube trays and melting into drinks.

And sitting right in the middle of the mayhem were his old *amigos*, Los Chimichangos.

"*Hola*, Skippito." Don Diego, the biggest of the small ones, grinned. "We have been waiting for you, dude."

"*Sí*, Skippito," said Poquito Tito. "Yesterday morning we left the house to buy some beans, and at night when we returned, a Bobble-ito was in *la casa perrito*."

"Not in the leetle doghouse!" exclaimed Skippito.

"Uh-huh," said Poquito Tito. "He's a fanatica, and so dramatica, and he bobbles and nods in our attica."

"He must be a pain in the sciatica," said Skippito.

"He's a yes man," added Don Diego.
And then all of the doggies nodded: Uh-huh, uh-huh, uh-huh, uh-huh.

"A jumbolito pain," agreed Polka Dot-ito. "And you are just what the dog-tor ordered."

This made the poochitos feel so good that they all began to sing and dance:

"First you turn the music way up loud,

Then you nod your head up and down

And wag your loco tail, back and forth,

To the chimichanga rumba

and the cha-cha-cha."

"Stop eet! You are keel-ing me, dudes!" said Skippito.

"Enough of the monkey beez-ness," said
Poquito Tito as he pulled Skippito outside
and over to a giant tortilla.

"Lie down and close your eyes,"
ordered Poquito Tito.
"*Porque?*" asked Skippito
nervously.

"Because, dude,"
said Poquito Tito, "at five o'clock
Abuelo Crispito will spill the
frijoles."

"Not the beans again,"
said Skippito.

At *cinco* bells, a Chihuahua as
old as Montezuma popped out
of the holey boulder and

"Pt-ooo-ey!"

brought forth three beans.
   "It's a three-beaner," declared
the *perritos*. Then they rolled
Skippito into a three-bean
burrito. "Now we are sure to
have good luck."

Then the burrito was packed onto the skateboard with the rest of the poochitos, and together they rolled over the cliff into the valley of the dogs, singing as they went.

"Yes, sirree sirrito,

(clap-clap)

It's the return of our boy,

El Skippito!

(clap-clap)

A bird in his ear

Said we needed him here.

It's Ka-boom!

To the big Bobble-ito!"

(clap-clap)

Los Chimichangos and the
burrito blew into the town of Pato
Pato Ganso faster than a flea on a flying
fur ball. To the right of the square stood *la casa
perrito.*

"*Mira*, Skippito," howled Don Diego. "The nodding
Bobble-ito is up in the attica."
But Skippito was too scared to look.

The *perritos* did not give a hootito about Skippito's jitters.
They just wanted the Bobble-ito out. And he was the dog for the job.

With one big flourish, the *perritos* unrolled the tortilla and
tossed the kitty boy and the beans

up

up

up   into the air until he landed
on the roof of the doghouse.

"Go get him, Skippito!" cried the poochitos.

"Oh,
MAMALITA!"
cried Skippito, catching a glimpse of
the hulking shadow of the Bobble-ito.

Oingy-Boingy Bouncy- **POUNCY**

Skippito flashed his naughty monkey eyes and lunged straight for the head of the Bobble-ito.

"YEE-HAW-ito!"
hollered Skippito as he took the ride of his life. And in no time flat, the kitty boy brought that Bobble-ito right down to size.

Faster than you could say "chili-chewing Chihuahuas," he grabbed the itty-bitty Bobble-ito and stuffed him into his pants.

Lickety-Splickety

Rickety-Tickety

Skippito rode the railing all the way down to the front door . . .

. . . and he bounced into the good night air, landing right in the middle of the fluffy white tortilla.

Los Chimichangos rolled Skippito up snug as a bug and began to chant,

"Muchas gracias,
       Skippy-dippy-dango,
Bye, Bobble-ito,
       boogie-woogie tango,
Muchos poochos,
       licky-sticky mango,
Gozo bozo,
       chimi-chimi-chango."

(One more time!)

And they carried the purr-ito all the way back to his room.

With *Quiz Kitties* over, Mama Junebug directed her ears toward Skippyjon's very quiet room.

"Hmm," mused Mama, "I wonder what he's up to."

She told the girls to go and take a peek.

"He's all wrapped up in his old white blankie," said Jezebel.

"And he's talking to my itty-bitty-kitty bobblehead," said Ju-Ju Bee.

"Maybe he's thinking Siamese," added Jilly Boo.

"Really?" asked Mama. "Oh, he's such a little crumb cake."

But Skippyjon Jones was not thinking
Siamese. He was still thinking Chihuahua.
   "Do you like mice and beans?" Skippyjon
asked the bobblehead. Then he touched the
itty-bitty-kitty's nose with the tip of his
blanket.

The bobblehead just nodded:

Uh-huh,
    uh-huh,
        uh-huh.

"Me, too," said Skippyjon Jones.